For Brenda, of course—M.M.

For Hillside Church and especially Allyn Carl—S.J. and L.F.

Text copyright © 2010 by Michael McGowan
Illustrations copyright © 2010 by Steve Johnson and Lou Fancher

Grateful acknowledgement is made to Hope Publishing Co. for permission to reprint an excerpt from
"Great Is Thy Faithfulness" by Thomas O. Chisolm and William Runyan, copyright © 1923, copyright renewed 1951
by Hope Publishing Co. All rights reserved. Hope Publishing Co., Carol Stream, IL 60188.

Visit us on the Web! www.randomhouse.com/kids

Educators and librarians, for a variety of teaching tools, visit us at www.randomhouse.com/teachers

Library of Congress Cataloging-in-Publication Data
McGowan, Michael.
Sunday is for God / by Michael McGowan ; illustrated by Lou Fancher and Steve Johnson.
1st ed.
p. cm.
Summary: A young boy describes the events and activities that make Sunday a special day.
ISBN 978-0-375-84188-0 (trade) — ISBN 978-0-375-94591-5 (glb)
[1. Sunday—Fiction. 2. Family life—Fiction. 3. Church—Fiction.] I. Fancher, Lou, ill.
II. Johnson, Steve, ill. III. Title.
PZ7.S65556Su 2010
[E]—dc22
2008048828

The text of this book is set in Belen.
The illustrations are rendered in acrylic and collage on paper.

MANUFACTURED IN CHINA
1 3 5 7 9 10 8 6 4 2
First Edition

Sunday is for God

BY **Michael McGowan**

PICTURES BY **Steve Johnson** and **Lou Fancher**

schwartz & wade books · new york

Weekdays are for school. Saturday's for having fun. But Sunday is the Lord's day. Sunday is for God. That's what Momma says.

"Momma's been calling you," I whisper to Brother. He's twelve, he likes his sleep, but that wakes him up. "Just kidding," I tell him when he's half out of bed.

He starts after me, but then Momma calls us, for real: "Come to breakfast, you two!"

We head down to breakfast in our pajamas.
There's the ham and sausage and good eggs
with plenty of salt, and biscuits and jelly and
I don't know what-all. "Eat up," says Momma.
"Can't keep the good Lord waiting."

I clean my plate and reach for another biscuit,
but Daddy says, "What are you kids waiting
for? Get yourselves ready." He looks at me.
"You remember how to knot your tie?"

"Yes, sir," I say.

First I have to button that starchy collar under my chin, and it feels awful stiff and tight. I can't get the ends of my tie right, so Brother, who's already dressed and fussing with his hair, helps me. Then he goes back to fussing with his hair some more.

I can work my own cuff links. Momma is calling again.

I put on my suit coat and run downstairs, Brother right behind me. My coat already feels too hot. Momma says we've got to look nice for church. I guess that's what the Lord wants, but I wish He didn't.

Sister can't find her glove and Baby is starting to cry and pulling at Papaw's flashy tie. We can hear the church bells going already. "We'll be late!" Momma says. We close the door behind us and we're finally on our way.

Everybody's out, walking to church. Old Miss Annie smiles at me. She never smiles but on Sunday. My friend Joey is up ahead with his momma and daddy.

"Can I go talk to Joey?" I ask Momma.

"Just for a minute," she says. I run and catch up with him. "Bet I can make you laugh in church," I say.

"Bet I make you laugh first," he says.

When we get to church, Momma calls me back. She straightens my tie and smiles at me—she's pretty when she smiles—and says, "You're a handsome young man, you know that? Going to look just like your daddy."

Inside, the pews are filling up. It's even hotter than outside. Church has a special smell—kind of like up in the attic at home, but with flowers in it. The ladies are all waving their fans, and the men are already wiping their foreheads with big old handkerchiefs, all different colors. Mr. McCallum is playing the organ. There's something he does, makes it sound like it's trembling. The choir starts to sing.

"Yes, we'll gather at the river,
The beautiful, the beautiful river."

It makes me wish I was down by the river right this minute, with my pants rolled up, wading in the cool clear water.

Papaw and the other deacons sit up by the altar. Some of them are wearing blue suits, and some of them are wearing gray suits, and some of them are wearing black suits, and the new deacon has a suit with stripes. They all have fancy ties like Papaw. Even though they're all sweating, they look happy to be there.

Brother Cartwright takes his place in front of them, in the pulpit.

> *"Gather with the saints at the river*
> *That flows by the throne of God."*

There's prayers and readings from the Bible. Babies are crying and little kids are twisting around every which way. My collar itches, but I'm not allowed to scratch. Brother fusses with his hair some more and Daddy tells him, "Stop that. The Lord don't mind how your hair looks."

I want to ask Daddy why the Lord wants us to get dressed up, then. But I know better.

And now church really gets going.
Brother Cartwright is preaching up a storm
and sweating like crazy and mopping at his
face. People are saying "Amen," so I say it
too, extra loud, just when everybody else
is quiet. Joey turns around. He almost
laughs, but he keeps it inside. Momma
gives me one of her looks.

Brother Cartwright is a little like the
star of a show. I can't take my eyes off him.
He's reading from the Bible now:

> *"If I take the wings of the morning,*
> *and dwell in the uttermost parts*
> *of the sea . . ."*

I'd like to have wings, and fly away, out of
the church, over the streets, down to the
river. The people would look so little.
Maybe that's how we look to the Lord.

"Search me, O God, and know my heart:
try me, and know my thoughts."

Does the Lord know what I've been thinking? Uh-oh. That's a little scary. I look around. Nobody else seems worried. Joey turns around all of a sudden and makes a face at me, but it's not a very funny face, and I don't much feel like laughing anyway.

Up by the altar, Papaw has his eyes shut but he's not asleep. He's listening hard, and every so often he nods his head, like he's saying, "Yes, sir, that's the truth."

"The Lord is nigh unto all that call upon Him;
He upholdeth all them that fall, and raiseth up
all those that be bowed down."

Sister asks me, "What is he saying?"

"I think he's saying the Lord will take care of us no matter what. Like Momma and Daddy."

Now everybody is saying "Amen" real loud. Brother Cartwright is done with his sermon, and it's time to dig the quarter out of my pocket for the collection. The deacons come around with the plates. They're not like regular plates. They're made out of wood and they have words carved on them, but the letters are different from regular letters and I can't read what they say. We all give a little bit, even Baby. But when Brother Cartwright gets the plates back, he says it's not enough, so we dig again. Then we all sing.

"Praise God from whom all blessings flow.
Praise Him, all creatures here below. . . ."

God is
you will be
be given
to see the
You hypocrite
your faithful
me.

Brother Cartwright comes back to the pulpit and prays. We bow our heads and I scratch under my collar a little bit, just a little bit, and I squeeze my eyes shut. "Bless my family, Lord," I pray. "Keep me safe. Jesus, help me be better in every way."

I can tell when Brother Cartwright is getting on toward the end of his prayer. His voice gets bigger and deeper, like he's going to make sure the Lord can hear him all the way up in Heaven. "Keep us, Lord, under the shadow of Thy wings."

I like the way that sounds. This time when I say "Amen" it's just a whisper.

When the last hymn comes, I know church is
getting to be over for this Sunday. Everybody's
smiling. We all sing as loud as we can,

"We're marching upward to Zion,
The beautiful city of God."

I'm real hungry, but I can hardly move for all the people. Joey and I push out to the sunlight. We won't get in too much trouble now that church is done. Brother is fussing with his hair again but nobody tells him to stop. I ask Momma, "Can I walk with Joey?" and she smiles, that pretty smile, and says, "Go on ahead."

a tent-cloth;
you have constructed your
upon the waters
There is an appointed time for
everything,
uproot the plant
dance.
and happy those wh
ways,
Happy the man watchin
gates,
waiting at my doo
or he who finds n
vigorates

We race all the way home, and I go inside and Joey goes on down the block to where he lives.

I whip off my tie and jacket but I stay in my clean white shirt. Daddy and Papaw do the same, and I roll up my sleeves just like they do. Papaw looks happy—not laughing and smiling happy, just quiet happy. Daddy looks like he's glad to be home.

Before we know it, Momma has Baby fed and dinner on the table. It's fried chicken and gravy and mashed potatoes and greens and corn bread, and it's all ready at the same time and it's all hot. The grown-ups drink iced tea. Brother asks for tea too, but Momma says no, so all the kids get ice water, like always. Papaw says grace, and he makes sure to get everybody in.

"Bless us and keep us in Jesus's name. Amen!"

We eat and we laugh and we talk. Finally Daddy says, "Momma, thank you for this fine meal." There's a knock on the door. Must be Joey.

"May I be excused?" I ask, and Daddy says, "You're excused."

Momma says, "You change your clothes before you go out to play, now."

Lo, I am about to create
Our love
have confidence on the
day of judgment;
And since fear has to do
because he first
he is a liar.

Sunday afternoon slips into Sunday evening. Tomorrow it will be a regular day. But today is special. Sunday is the Lord's day. Sunday is for God.